Jonathan Ames

YOU WERE NEVER REALLY HERE

Jonathan Ames is the author of the novels *I Pass Like Night*, *The Extra Man*, and *Wake Up, Sir!*, the graphic novel *The Alcoholic* (illustrated by Dean Haspiel), and the essay collections *What's Not to Love?*, *My Less Than Secret Life*, *I Love You More Than You Know*, and *The Double Life Is Twice as Good*. He is the editor of *Sexual Metamorphosis: An Anthology of Transsexual Memoirs* and has been awarded a Guggenheim Fellowship. He is also the creator of two television shows: the HBO series *Bored to Death* and the STARZ series *Blunt Talk*. On both shows, in addition to being the creator, he was the showrunner and executive producer. Several years ago, he had two boxing matches, fighting as "The Herring Wonder."

YOU
WERE
NEVER
REALLY
HERE

Jonathan Ames

VINTAGE CRIME/BLACK LIZARD

Vintage Books

A Division of Penguin Random House LLC

New York

FIRST VINTAGE CRIME/BLACK LIZARD EDITION, MARCH 2018

All rights reserved. Published in the United States by Vintage Books,
a division of Penguin Random House LLC, New York, and
distributed in Canada by Random House of Canada, a division of
Penguin Random House Canada Limited, Toronto. Originally
published in slightly different form as an original eBook by
Byliner Inc., San Francisco, in 2013.

Vintage is a registered trademark and Vintage Crime/Black Lizard
and colophon are trademarks of Penguin Random House LLC.

Library of Congress Cataloging-in-Publication Data
Names: Ames, Jonathan, author.
Title: You were never really here / Jonathan Ames.
Description: First Vintage Crime/black lizard edition. |
New York : Vintage Books, 2018.
Identifiers: LCCN 2017037748| ISBN 9780525562894 (trade pbk.) |
ISBN 9780525562900 (ebook)
Classification: LCC PS3551.M42 Y68 2018 | DDC 813/.54—dc23
LC record available at https://lccn.loc.gov/2017037748

**Vintage Crime/Black Lizard Trade Paperback
ISBN: 978-0-525-56289-4
eBook ISBN: 978-0-525-56290-0**

Book design by Christopher M. Zucker

www.blacklizardcrime.com

Printed in the United States of America
10 9 8 7 6 5 4 3 2 1

For Amy Grace Loyd

YOU
WERE
NEVER
REALLY
HERE

Joe felt something behind him. It was the presence of life and the coming of violence, and that anticipation, that sensitivity, enabled him to turn in time and catch the blackjack on his shoulder, which was better than taking it on the back of his head.

Also, it was his left shoulder and Joe was right-handed, and, turning around completely, he was able to grab the man's wrist before the blackjack came down again, and they were face to face, the same height, and Joe immediately drove his forehead, like a brick, into the bridge of the man's nose, shattering the bone, and the man, his eyes blinded by red pain, began to fall, and Joe brought up his knee, brought it up hard, without mercy, into the man's jaw, breaking it.

The man went down completely, strings cut, lifeless but breathing.

Joe quickly swung his head to the left and the right. He was in an alley wide enough for a car. He'd come out of his flop hotel's service entrance in the middle of the passageway, and no one was walking by or had stopped at either end. No one had seen. There was street light coming from the avenue, but the alley was mostly in shadow.

Joe wiggled his left arm, trying to get life into it, the blackjack had numbed the whole limb, and he dragged the body behind a dumpster and quickly went through the pockets of the light coat, a blue windbreaker. The fallen was a pro. No wallet. No ID. Just keys and a money clip with about two hundred dollars. But there was a cell phone. So he wasn't a total professional. He didn't anticipate losing, and he didn't anticipate being hunted, like Joe did. Joe never carried a cell phone.

Joe looked at the blackjack. Police issue. Probably a bent cop from the Cincinnati suburbs doing a little moonlighting in the big town, where his face wasn't known. Whoever had sent him didn't want Joe dead. Not yet, anyway. They wanted to bring him in, talk to him. There was probably a partner waiting in a car, waiting for a call. Joe would have been spooked by a car in the alley, so this one had hidden in a cove of a doorway. He'd sap Joe and call his partner. They'd throw his body in the car and bring him to the boss. That had been the plan. It didn't work.

Joe looked at the last text message sent: "Keep engine running. We'll want to move quick." "Copy" was the reply. Probably two bent cops.

The alley went one way. That meant the partner would be to the left, idling, so he could pull right in, not circle the block. Joe hesitated. He was ready to leave Cincinnati. He had done his job. Extracted the girl. He didn't need to take out the one in the car. His informant had given him up, gave them his hotel, even his use of the service entrance, but that's all they could have gotten, because that's all the informant had.

Joe thought about what was in his room: a toothbrush, a new hammer, a bag, and a change of clothes. But nothing important, nothing identifiable. He had been heading out to get something to eat and was going to leave tomorrow, but he should have left as soon as the job was done. *Sloppy*, he thought. *What the fuck is wrong with me?*

Soon the one in the car would come looking. Joe didn't want any more fights, because you didn't win every fight. Joe figured they just wanted to know how he had gotten to them and if others would follow, and then they would have killed him. But he didn't need to take them all out because they wanted information. He was just one man. Not the complete arm of justice. *I did enough*, he thought. *The girl is damaged but free.*

So he ran the opposite way down the alley, darted his head out fast, looking to his left and right—there wasn't a third man guarding that end. Nobody sitting in a car, nobody planted in a doorway trying not to look like a plant. He stepped out into the street, started to walk. It was late October and there was a sweet smell in the air, like a flower that had just died. He thought about a time when he'd been happy. It had been more than two decades.

Then Joe spotted a green cab. He liked the cabs in Cincy. The cars were old and the drivers were old. It felt like the past. He got in.

"Airport," he said, and he fingered the money clip. He'd give the driver a nice tip.

Joe lay in bed in his mother's house. He thought about committing suicide. Such thinking was like a metronome for him. Always present, always ticking. All day long, every few minutes, he'd think, *I have to kill myself.*

But in the mornings and before going to bed, the thinking was more elaborate. He knew it was a waste of time—it was going to have to wait till his mother passed—but he couldn't stop. It was his favorite story. The only one he knew the ending of for sure.

The past few weeks it always involved water. His plan of late was to slip into the Hudson at night, during high tide, by the Verrazano. The currents were strong, and he would be taken out to sea. He didn't want anyone to be bothered with the body.

Once, when he first got out of the Marines, long before he had gone back to live with his mother, he had nearly done it. He had been processed out of Marine Corps base Quantico and ended up in a motel near Baltimore, drinking by himself for a few days and going to a movie theater, seeing the same three pictures over and over. Then one night in the motel, he had taken a lot of sleeping pills and wrapped his head in a few layers of black plastic bags, duct-taping them around his neck. He felt himself diminishing, a shadow around the edges of his mind, and he heard a voice say, *It's all right, you can go, you were never really here.*

But then he clawed off the bags and pumped his own stomach. After that, the story never involved leaving a body behind, leaving a mess behind. That was shameful. When it was time to be removed, that's what it would be—a complete erasure. So the sea would have him. It wouldn't mind one more piece of waste. He had nowhere else to turn.

He heard his mother downstairs and got out of bed. He did one hundred push-ups and one hundred sit-ups. His morning ritual. That, walking a great deal, and squeezing a handball as often as possible was all he did for exercise. He especially liked his hands to be

strong. It was good in a fight. You break your adver-
sary's fingers, you have an immediate advantage. It
frightened even the hardest men to have their fingers
snapped, and in a fight, like a dance, you often held
hands.

So his hands were weapons, his whole body was
a weapon, cruel like a baseball bat. Six-two, 190, no
fat. He was forty-eight, but his olive-colored skin was
still smooth, which made him appear younger than
he was. His jet-black hair had receded at the temples,
leaving a little wedge, like the point of a knife, at the
front. He kept his hair at the length of a Marine on
leave.

He was half-Irish, half-Italian. He had a long,
twisting Italian nose and eerie Gaelic blue eyes, set
back and deep, Italian but for their color. It was a
mournful face, a self-involved face, with a thick forehead, another weapon, and his jaw was too big and
long, like the blade of a shovel. When he passed security cameras, he tucked it in. The black baseball hat
that he wore most of the time hid the rest of his face,
which in its entirety was not ugly but not handsome.
It was something else. It was a mask he would tear off
if he could. He was aware that he was not completely
sane, so he kept himself in rigid check, playing both
jailer and prisoner.

He put on pants and a T-shirt and went down to

the kitchen for breakfast. His mother sat in her chair by the window in her housedress and slippers, waiting for him, patient and still, intent only on watching the door for his arrival. His plate was set. She was eighty, very short now, and had the look of a Mediterranean widow. In Genoa, where she was born, she'd be dressed in black, the widows there turning into nuns of a sort during the quiet, protracted ends of their lives.

Her silver-gray hair was piled in a knot on her head, and she wore large glasses that took up most of her sallow face, which was round and sad. Her hair, uncut for years, when set free, reached all the way to her waist. Joe had seen her once in the bathroom in her housedress—the door was slightly ajar—and her head was in the sink, she was giving herself a shampoo, and then she had risen up and thrown her hair back, like a young woman, and the hair snapped out in an arc like a long silvery rope. It struck him as magnificent. She had been beautiful once.

She got up slowly to pour his coffee and make his eggs. Behind her glasses, she looked at him with love, a slight flicker in her eyes, but she didn't smile. That look was the only joy in his life and her only joy as well. They hardly ever spoke.

————

As he did every day around two p.m., Joe left their house in Rego Park and went for a walk, tacking thirty blocks west, following a different meandering route each time but always running parallel to Queens Boulevard. Eventually he would pass, at Sixty-third Drive, Angel's #1 Bodega, which was Joe's answering service. If McCleary wanted to get in touch he called Angel, and Angel, following Joe's instructions, each time put the same sign in the window, with the same misspelling, for Joe to see: "Egg and Bacons Sandwich $1.50." Angel didn't know Joe's name or where he lived, which kept Angel safe and which kept Joe safe.

Joe was thinking, though, that he needed a new service. The only time he interacted with Angel, after their initial meeting, was to buy a pint of milk once a month, leaving five hundred dollars hidden in the refrigerator. Sometimes Angel's son—a fourteen-year-old named Moises—was there when he bought the milk. Moises, tall and skinny, ready for his last bit of growth, was a smart kid, noticed everything, and Joe felt that Angel had told the boy something, though he warned him not to.

Then a week ago, just before he left for the Cincy job, Joe was going into his mother's house, using the back entrance off the alleyway where each house had a small stand-alone garage. Joe never went in the front door, and hardly anyone ever saw him going into the house—the alleyway was mostly deserted, and Joe had a way of moving quickly and nearly invisibly—but as he unlocked the back door, removing the small cardboard wedges that let him know if the door had been opened while he was gone, he felt something and looked behind him.

Moises had just come onto the second-story fire escape of a house across the alley and was looking right at Joe. Then Moises's friend came onto the escape—they were going to smoke cigarettes—and Joe slipped inside. With all the countless dwellings between Joe and Angel's bodega, it was bad luck that Moises should have a friend who lived just across the way.

The signal to call McCleary was in the window, but Joe went into the shop to talk to Angel. He tucked in his shovel-jaw and lowered the brim of his hat so that the security cameras couldn't record his face. He was wearing a tan Carhartt jacket, a blue T-shirt, jeans, and steel-tipped work boots. All his clothing was old and worn. He looked like any of the thousands of laborers and construction workers who alternately build up and tear down the city. It was good cover.

Angel was behind the deli counter, and when he saw Joe he stiffened, looked nervous. It wasn't the end of the month. It wasn't time to get paid. They went into the back room. Angel was short and fat and looked like a liar, but he was a good man, which was why Joe had chosen him.

"Did your son tell you he saw me?" Joe didn't make small talk. The more he talked, the more someone might know him, and the more someone knew him, experienced him, the greater the chance they could be damaged.

Angel instinctively cowered, his back against the metal shelving of extra stock. He hesitated. The five hundred dollars a month was a blessing, but maybe too good a blessing.

"Yes, sir," Angel said, coming out with it. Joe seemed to warrant a military response, though Angel had never served.

"Did he tell you *where* he saw me?"

"No, sir, I told him 'Don't tell me.' I knew you wouldn't want me to know. My son don't mean to see you. He's a good boy."

Joe looked at him. Angel wasn't lying. Joe gave a slight shrug of resignation and closed his eyes slowly and gently, almost as if he was going to fall asleep standing up. It was a semaphore, Joe's way of saying good-bye. Then he left the back room without speaking, moving in the liquid way that he had, and he headed for McCleary's. He didn't plan on seeing Angel ever again. It was no longer secure.

Joe sat across from McCleary battered desk between th cramped office on the top on Thirty-eighth Street and Eighth hattan. He was on a long, winding hallway of tier accountants, insurance agents, real estate lifers, coin experts, and Medicare dentists. His window looked onto the air shaft, with a fraction of the sky visible above the roof of the adjoining building. Joe glanced at an odd series of clouds. They looked like the X-rays of rotten teeth.

McCleary was finishing up a call—he had been on the phone when Joe came in—and, using a pencil, was pushing around the dead cigarettes in his ashtray. They were twisted and tormented looking, crushed little worms. Every few seconds he said, "Yeah . . . yeah . . . yeah."

Many of the big security outfits and white-shoe law firms used McCleary as a middleman for the blacklist freelancers. This kept things off their books, showing only a payment to McCleary, who was clean. Jobs that called for illegal tactics were then farmed out by McCleary to men like Joe, who were paid in cash, and a very specific kind of job was almost always given only to Joe.

...leary was in his mid-sixties, an ex–state
...r and ex-PI with the hideous, vein-ruptured
...e of a whiskey drinker. He was a big, loose man
...one to seed. His cheap gray suit hung on him like
jowls. His fat sausage fingers were clubbed—his yellow fingernails floated above the tips of his fingers, a
hard brown substance, from beneath, pushing them
up. No oxygen reached the end of McCleary's limbs.
He had been smoking cigarettes longer than he had
been drinking whiskey. Joe tortured himself, imagin-
ing what McCleary's toes must look like. He thought
of putting them in his mouth. Joe hated his own mind.
He wished he could be put down like a dog.

Like a lot of hard drinkers, McCleary hadn't lost
any of his wood-brown hair, and none of it was gray,
which made his veined, pink-red face all the more
obscene. He was a rotting husk of something that
had once been powerful, but he could still man a desk
and run off-the-books operatives. He grunted into the
phone and looked at Joe, letting him know he was
almost done.

McCleary liked Joe, but he didn't have much to
work with. Joe played it closer to the vest than any
cop or dick or con he had ever met. An FBI agent
named Goulden with big-time credentials had sent
him Joe and a partial dossier two years ago. That's all
he really had. He wondered if he liked Joe because

he looked Italian. McCleary's wife had been Italian, and hardly a minute went by that he didn't think of her. Somehow she had died before he did. They never had children. He wished he could have given her that gift. Maybe she would have lived. McCleary grunted one more time and started to lower the phone.

"Get rid of Angel's number," Joe said as the phone hit the cradle. "I'll find a new service."

"Okay, no problem," said McCleary, glancing at his Rolodex, where he kept the number. He was old-fashioned, he mostly relied on pen and paper, but he also had a computer, a nice laptop. You couldn't keep up if you didn't. "How was Cincinnati?"

Joe closed his eyes and nodded, hoping that would pass as some kind of answer. He knew that the agency would have been paid by the client, followed by McCleary getting his cut soon enough and then Joe would get his, and so what more was there to say? He certainly wasn't going to tell McCleary about the bent cop in the alleyway. That slipup embarrassed Joe.

McCleary looked at him. *The bastard's going to sleep again*, McCleary thought. He always wished Joe might open up so they could talk a little shop—McCleary missed being in the field—but he knew it was hopeless. But damn it, the guy had to crack someday. He was going to wait him out this time.

"Why am I here?" Joe asked, opening his eyes, moving things along.

McCleary sighed, giving up, and then launched into it: "This is a job I got directly, so we'll split the money, which is good. Maybe I'll go to Peter Luger's just for the hell of it. Anyway, you know State Senator Votto? For a while, in the eighties, I ran his security detail when I was a trooper."

Joe nodded. Votto had been a big power broker in Albany for decades, but because of massive corruption and ties to the mob, which had finally come to light after years of rumors, he had been removed from office and arraigned. While awaiting his trial, free on bail, he died in his sleep, avoiding judgment and conviction. An aneurysm burst in his brain, and he never knew he was gone.

McCleary continued: "Well, his son, Albert, called me. Now *he's* a big shot in Albany. Got elected a year ago and right away they started saying he could be governor. All you need in politics is name recognition, even if the name is shit. But then six months ago, his daughter, thirteen years old, went missing. Supposedly a pervert off the Internet got her, but you know what that means, and the wife committed suicide a month later, couldn't deal with it, which is too much tragedy. He won't be able to run for governor for a while, but then in a few years it'll probably get him the sympathy vote. You read about it in the paper?"

"Yeah," Joe said.

"Well, he thinks he's got a lead on the girl. Said he doesn't want to go to the cops. He didn't give me much else. He knows the drill. I'm the clean middle-man. He drove down from Albany this morning. He's staying at the W downtown, near Wall Street, near the money. Wants to see you now."

"Okay," Joe said. He stood up and headed for the door.

"Try to be sociable, a little chitchat won't kill you," said McCleary. "I knew his father. He was a crook, but half-decent in his own way."

Joe nodded and left, moving soundlessly.

"Come by next week and I'll give you your money for the Cincinnati job, maybe we could get a drink," McCleary shouted after him in a rush, feeling needy and old, but the door had closed and he didn't know if Joe had heard. McCleary wondered at himself, not understanding why he had suggested a drink, except maybe to let the air out of his loneliness, like releasing a prayer that would never be heard.

Joe took the stairs down, eight flights. He avoided ele-vators if he could. They were dangerous boxes in every way—coffins with cameras and only one way out.

As Joe descended rapidly, his body an agile and almost ageless machine, he thought about McCleary, whom he genuinely liked. He had heard what McCleary had shouted after him and wished he could drink a beer with him, watch a baseball game, but he couldn't allow himself such things anymore. Not for some time now. Not since he had found the girls in the truck and something in his mind had broken, like a floorboard giving way. And from beneath that floorboard in his mind there came this all-consuming self-hatred, which had always been there and which he could no longer suppress.

What Joe didn't grasp was that his sense of self had been carved, like a totem, by his father's beatings. The only way for Joe to have survived his father's sadism was to believe that he deserved it, that it was justified, and that belief was still with him and could never be undone. In essence, he had been waiting nearly fifty years to finish the job that his father had started.

Joseph Sr., also a Marine, had fought in the Korean War. He went in human and came out subhuman. After his discharge with honors, he found work at La Guardia Airport as a mechanic but felt that it was beneath him. So he hated his job, hated his life, hated the constant nightmares of being in battle without cover or ammunition, and he hated his beautiful Italian wife because she loved him and he couldn't feel it. They had married before the war, before he had been changed, destroyed.

His response was to drink heavily and with great

Irish tolerance, but there was no peace in his mind no matter how much he put down. Joe was born after his mother had had three miscarriages, most likely brought on by his father's hands.

To help himself with his rage, Joseph Sr. had fashioned half a broom handle with which to beat Joe, primarily on the body. This was after a priest at Joe's school, when Joe was eight, had taken note of Joe's black eye and split lip and told Joseph Sr. to go easy on the child, that corporal punishment should never involve the face. So he had sawed a broom handle in half and wrapped it with black electrical tape. Joe, from this crude baton, still had notches on his shins, grooves that he liked to trace with his fingers, a private ritual he always engaged in before putting on his socks.

Joe's mother tried, but she couldn't stop her husband, just as Joe, too small and weak, couldn't stop his father from beating her.

When Joe was thirteen, his father, very drunk, wasn't able, one time, to find the broom handle and so had come at him with a hammer instead. Joe fell, trying to get away, and as he crawled he lost consciousness, fainting from terror. He woke up a few minutes later in urine-soaked pants and his father was smiling at him and laughing, white spit in the corners of his mouth like battery acid.

A month later, Joseph Sr. died, choking on his own

blood from burst esophageal ulcers, a heavy drinker's death, but that didn't seem to change things much for Joe and his mother. Even after they put him in the ground, they seemed to be waiting always for him to return.

Senator Votto was a big man, bigger than Joe, but he was soft and heavy. He was wearing an expensive gray suit and a red tie that looked like a streak of blood down the middle of his chest. He had a full head of hair, like most politicians, and he had a bland, fleshy American face. It was as if the Italian in him, the Votto in him, had been bleached out. Because of his size he was garrulous and cocky, which made him a good candidate, a good politician, but as with most sons of powerful men, if you looked closely, there was a weakness to his face and a petty cruelty. A different kind of shadow followed him than followed Joe.

"McCleary said you were ex-FBI and ex–Marine Corps."

"That's correct," said Joe. They were in the living room of Votto's suite. Votto was on the couch, Joe on a hard chair pulled over from the desk. A sleek coffee table was between them. The W was modern and uncomfortable and smelled like a spa, like scented candles—the effete odor of new wealth. Joe had been forced to take the elevator, no access to the stairs from the lobby, and so he was a little on edge.

"Were you in Iraq or Afghanistan?" Votto was playing the senator, a smart man who asks smart, to-the-point questions of inferiors.

"Saudi Arabia, Kuwait, and Iraq. The first war. Ninety-one."

Votto was momentarily thrown. He had miscalculated Joe's age. The unlined face. Then he said, "Nobody died in that one, right?"

Joe closed his eyes. Votto was ignorant. But most people were. Joe had been part of the first ground assault in Khafji, Saudia Arabia. He had lost eleven friends and was credited with eighteen kills. Joe opened his eyes. He said, "Yeah, nobody died."

Votto, despite his own terrible problems, smiled reflexively in a Pavlovian way. He was not a deep thinker. It was reassuring to know that America sometimes fought good wars.

"And what did you do in the FBI?"

Joe knew that clients needed to ask questions, that vetting him in this way gave them a sense of control, even if it was illusory, because, of course, there was no control. Not for anybody. But he had ready answers to put the client at ease. For the job, whether with the people who were paying or with the people he had to go through, he could make conversation. It wasn't personal. There was an objective. He was an instrument. He had a use and could let his mask speak almost freely. He could play-act normalcy of a kind.

"For twelve years I worked undercover, part of a sex-trafficking task force," he said. "The victims were mostly women and children brought over from other countries and forced into the sex trade. There were also the children, already living in the States, who were baited on the Internet and kidnapped. Some boys, mostly girls. All of them sex slaves. That was my beat. The last few years I've been working with McCleary, doing more or less the same thing."

Votto nodded, was quiet now. He had taken in what Joe said and seemed distracted, in pain. There was sweat on his upper lip and at the line of his hair. The room was cool. Votto's phone, on the coffee table, buzzed. He stared at it, lost. Didn't pick the thing up. It stopped buzzing. Joe wanted to move the conversation along. He said, "McCleary told me that your daughter went missing after meeting a man online."

Votto's phone buzzed again. He picked it up this time. Read an e-mail. Put the phone back down on the table. "Sorry," he said. "*Albany.*" He spoke the name of the state capital like it was a poison.

"Right," Joe said. He started over: "So your daughter went missing after meeting a man online?"

Votto didn't answer. He looked away, stood up, and went to the small refrigerator, hidden in a cupboard, and removed a bottle of club soda and a mini-bar Jack Daniel's.

With his back to Joe, he poured some soda into a glass and emptied the whiskey. He didn't offer to make Joe a drink. He took a slug, kept his back to Joe, and then said, "Yeah, it was some guy she met on Facebook. Thirty years old, looked like a male model. And she was mature for her age. They say it's hormones in the food. She was thirteen and already boy crazy, but the thirty-year-old didn't exist. Was somebody else's picture. They don't know who she met. The cops got nowhere. She vanished. My wife couldn't take it."

Joe let that hang a moment. Then he said, "How were things at home with your daughter before this happened?"

Votto took another slug and then turned. In a small voice he said, "She hardly spoke to her mother and she hated me. A phase, I guess." Votto, ashamed, his eyes lowered, came back to the couch and sat down. Then he looked up at Joe, like you look at a priest—*Will you forgive me?*

Joe arranged his face and body—he widened his eyes, tilted his head, and raised his shoulders; all of it meant to signify sympathy and a deep resignation. This was a face and posture that his mother made often. It occurred to him that he was increasingly borrowing the gestures of an old woman slipping into dementia, an old woman, nearly deaf, who communicated with him like they were both in a silent movie.

Then he reassembled himself and pressed on with what was essential: "McCleary said that you had new information but that you didn't want to go to the police. Did your daughter contact you?"

"No," he said. "I got some kind of anonymous text this morning. I checked with the phone company. Came off one of those quick phones you can buy. They're untraceable. You don't even get the place where it was bought."

Joe sometimes, out of necessity, used such phones, but mostly steered clear of them. He didn't like his voice to be recorded, and he assumed that all conversations were. His goal, always, was to leave as little imprint of himself as possible, wherever he went, whatever he did.

"Let me see the text," Joe said.

Votto picked up his phone, played with it, handed it to Joe. Joe read the message:

> *Your daughter is in new york in a brothel at 244 east 48th street. I couldn't live with myself if i didn't let you know. She wants to come home. I don't think she knows about your wife i'm so*

sorry. I can't go to the police for obvious reasons.
So i'm letting you know. They have her on drugs
but she looks ok i'm sorry with all my heart.

"Gotta be legit, right?" said Votto, suddenly agitated. The little bit of booze and the circumstances were starting to work on him. "Couldn't be a hoax, right? He really saw her." He drank the rest of his drink. His face was getting flushed.

Joe read the text several times quickly. There was an odd quality to it, but it also made sense. Sounded like the person was coming down off drugs—remorseful and paranoid. Men who requested underage girls were often on cocaine or crystal meth, and not all of them were full-blown sociopaths. Some of them experienced regret.

Joe put the phone on the coffee table. The text was sent at 7:23 this morning. The guy had bought the phone at 7:00, as soon as the store, probably a Rite Aid, opened. Waited a few minutes. Screwed up his courage. Sent the text. Threw the phone away.

"It's worth looking into," Joe said. "Often the way the prostitution rings come after young girls is to create a fake profile on websites like Facebook. Pictures of a handsome guy is the lure, the bait. And that might be what happened to your daughter."

Joe didn't add that they also targeted the children

who revealed themselves, usually during an exchange of messages, to be very unhappy.

"Do you think whoever sent that text fucked her?" Votto's neck was suddenly very red.

Joe didn't answer that. "Why did you call McCleary and not the police?"

"Fuck the police." Votto stood up, started pacing. His jugular vein looked like a worm. "The cops haven't done shit!" He went back to the minibar, took out a mini-vodka, and downed the thing, then choked and coughed, bending over. He wasn't a drinker, but he was trying to act like one. Joe just watched.

Then Votto gathered himself, his voice hoarse: "I don't want to mess around with the police, with warrants. I don't want to waste time. I want you to go there and get her. And then I want to find out from her who she saw and take care of the bastard myself. It's got to be somebody I know. Somebody I know *fucked* my daughter!"

The whole thing felt like a performance to Joe, and Votto, trying to show that he was a man, an angry man, took a swipe at the thin modern lamp on the desk. It skittered across the desk's surface, but, hung up on its cord, it fell pathetically, ineffectively, not even breaking. Then Votto slumped back down onto the couch, lowered his head, and started crying.

Joe leaned forward, unmoved, and stroked the

divots in his right shin. Votto wanted to take the law into his own hands, but not for his daughter's sake. He wanted to find the man, maybe a friend, who knew his cell-phone number. He wanted to find the man, maybe a friend, who had raped his daughter.

Joe realized later, tragically, that he should have walked out at that moment. But he didn't. He was thinking it wasn't the girl's fault that her father was a weak fool. He let Votto cry some more and then said, "Do you have a picture of her?"

Votto lifted up his wet, porcine face. He was a fat little boy. He removed from his wallet a school snapshot, his daughter's eighth-grade yearbook picture, and handed it to Joe.

"Her name's Lisa. Did I mention that?"

It was almost 5:30, and Joe, using a credit card that matched one of his identities (he had three), rented a car from Enterprise, which had a branch in a garage on Thompson Street near Washington Square Park. Before getting in the car, he slipped on a pair of surgical gloves—he always carried a small packet of them, like a nurse, but for other reasons.

Then he drove the car to a hardware store on Twenty-ninth Street. There weren't too many left in Manhattan. He took off the gloves, not wanting to attract attention, and, touching only their disposable packaging, picked up duct tape and a cutting razor. He also got a new hammer, being careful to grasp only the cardboard sleeve on its handle.

Back at the car, he put the gloves on, got inside, and held the hammer in his hand. It fit nicely. A hammer was Joe's favorite weapon. He was his father's son, after all.

Also, a hammer left very little evidence, was excellent in close quarters, and seemed to frighten *everyone*. It held some universal place of terror in the human mind. The unexpected sight of it raised in Joe's hand would always momentarily paralyze his enemies, and those few seconds of paralysis were usually all that he needed. Joe also liked the common fire ax for this reason, but you couldn't conceal an ax. He put the hammer in the large front pocket of his jacket and drove to Forty-eighth Street.

The building was a three-story brownstone, on a street of brownstones. It was a mostly old-fashioned block, bookended by modern apartment towers, one at Third Avenue and one at Second Avenue. Joe circled the block several times and then double-parked, putting on his blinkers. If he saw a cop car enter the street by Third Avenue, he would resume circling. If he was lucky, which he would be eventually, though it might take a few hours, he would get a parking spot.

It was early evening, already dark out, and he hoped to make his move sometime after midnight. He had picked up two large bottles of water, one of which he emptied to use as a toilet.

All the windows of the brownstone were sealed tight by metal curtains, ensuring privacy. It was a premium brothel in a neighborhood of such places—it was close to the United Nations and Midtown's centers of corporate wealth. A connected realtor most likely rented it to the Russian or Italian mob, the two largest purveyors of high-end prostitution, which sometimes included the sale of underage girls, for which there was more than enough demand.

In New York City there were nearly 700,000 millionaires who were men. There were 250,000 each in Chicago and Los Angeles, and plenty more in the other large to midsize cities. If 0.5 percent   half a percentage point—of these men throughout the country were sexually and socially deviant in their desire for young girls, which would be a conservative estimate, then there was abundant incentive in the marketplace to provide what they wanted. One hour with a pretty twelve-, thirteen-, or fourteen-year-old white female cost anywhere from five to ten thousand dollars, and the more that was charged, the more the men wanted it, which was basic economics. It was a highly risky but very lucrative business.

Generally, at the top places, if they offered young girls, there were usually only one or two who had been properly Stockholmed. It wasn't an easy process to get these girls functional and productive, and a brothel that offered them—mixing them in with legal-aged women—was known on the street as a "playground." To avoid exposure and capture, the young girls were moved from city to city, working a network of playgrounds for a week or two at a time. These children usually lasted about two years before they were killed and thrown away, ensuring their silence, but during their twenty-four months of work, if they were properly run, they could bring in hundreds of thousands of dollars.

Joe had become very good at exfiltrating some of these girls, once he tracked them down, using methods that the police couldn't get away with. Normally, Joe had time to plan his approach and tactics, but this Votto case was of the moment and required him to fly more blind than he liked. Still, at his core, Joe was a Marine, and he had been well trained, as their motto went, to *adapt, improvise, and overcome.*

After a few hours of circling and occasionally double-parking, he got a spot fifteen yards from the brothel with excellent sight lines. There had been nothing for him to act on—he saw black town cars and SUVs drop men off and pick them up, and he saw one slender twenty-something girl in sweatpants and a pink ski jacket leave the brownstone, done for the night, but he didn't tail her. He was waiting for something better to work with, and it was still too early. He needed fewer people on the streets. So he sat in his car and went into a fugue state of sorts—simultaneously alert and peaceful.

Goulden was right, Joe thought. Work was good for him, relaxing. It was five years ago that he had first come undone. He found the thirty dead Chinese girls—poisoned by carbon monoxide—in the back of a refrigerated meat truck. If he had gotten there fifteen minutes sooner, just fifteen, they would have lived. What he saw was a holocaust pile of lifeless young women, frozen in their terror, huddled as they were in the back of the truck, trying to hide from the hose that had been lodged at the front. Their captors, knowing the FBI was closing in, had made sure there would be no survivors, no evidence that could *talk*.

It was then that the gears in his mind had turned on themselves—his limit for trauma, a very high limit, had finally been reached—and he went AWOL. He followed his usual pattern for hiding, and on the outskirts of Milwaukee, he holed up in a motel for two weeks in a state of deep paranoia, until he came up with a plan, a solution, a way to live, which was to get very small and very quiet and leave no wake. So he had to be pure. He had to be holy. He had to be contained.

He had come to believe that he was the recurring element—the deciding element—in all the tragedies experienced by the people he encountered. So if he could minimize his impact and his responsibility, then there was the chance, the slight chance, that there would be no more suffering for others. It was a negative grandiose delusion—narcissism inverted into self-hatred, a kind of autoimmune disorder of his psyche—but there was an undeniable element of truth to Joe's paranoiac state: where he went, pain and punishment followed.

To accomplish his goal of containment and purity, he couldn't let anyone near him. He had to abandon all friendships and give up on women. Women had always broken against him anyway, hidden as he was, especially from himself. They thought they could get near him, but it had never been possible. Still, he had tried for years, hoping each time that he might be capable of love. Then, after finding the girls in the truck, it was clear to him that everything had to stop. No more women, no more sex, no more companionship of any kind. He would speak as little as possible to the outside world, and so he went to his mother, the only person he could be trusted not to hurt. He returned to the house where he had grown up in

Queens. His father could still be felt in every room, and Joe got worse, not better.

The FBI jettisoned him for going AWOL, and for three years he and his mother lived in near silence and isolation. She didn't ask him why he had come home in his forties or what had happened. She knew it must not be good, but mostly she was just happy to have her Joseph back in the house.

Then, two years ago, Goulden came and found him and sent him to McCleary, hoping it would rehabilitate Joe. Goulden had always outranked him—first in the Marines and then in the FBI—so Joe did what his friend said. He went back to work. He found that he could still function exceedingly well as a weapon, and he had never stopped living as if he was still undercover. It had become a permanent state.

So it was a seamless return, and he didn't question things anymore if it was related to the job. He now thought of it as a level playing field. Everyone shared responsibility—on both sides of the moral axis—and he was of use. A hammer doesn't ask why it strikes.

A little after one a.m., Joe got what he needed from the brothel—the towel boy emerged, sent out on an errand. Joe moved fast. The towel boy, in jeans and a thick, hooded sweatshirt, was on the south side of the street, in the middle of the block, heading for Second Avenue. Joe didn't think he was security. They usually wore dark blazers and even ties to give the well-heeled johns a sense of comfort and class, as well to keep them in their place, to let them know that authority was present.

So Joe loped down the north side of the street and then crossed, five yards ahead of his target. He looked about. No immediate witnesses. It was a cold October night. Not too many people were out. He stepped from between two cars and right into the path of the towel boy—a thirty-two-year-old white man, a failed blackjack dealer from Atlantic City named Paul, who didn't have much talent for anything. He was startled by Joe's sudden appearance, and Joe shot out his right hand unerringly and grabbed Paul by the throat, the way a man might grab a woman's wrist. Paul didn't even have time to be scared. He was already half-dead. Everything Joe did was to establish immediate and complete dominance.

He then whispered, "Everything is going to be all right. I won't hurt you for long, I promise." With that, he let go of Paul's throat and threw a short, vicious punch into his diaphragm, doubling him over, and Joe put his arm around him. If anyone looked out a window, they'd see Joe helping his sick, gasping friend who'd had too much to drink. They'd see him guid-

ing the poor drunk across the street and into the backseat of his car.

Joe then shoved Paul across the seat and pulled
the door closed behind him. He made quick work
with the duct tape and cutting razor. He bound Paul's
wrists behind his back and taped his ankles together.
He had left the driver-side window open a crack so
that they wouldn't steam things up.

Paul's eyes were starting to focus, and he was gasping a little less audibly. Joe had him sit up straight, and
he rubbed Paul's shoulders. He wanted Paul to be of
use as quickly as possible.

"How many security are inside?" Joe asked.

Paul was too frightened to answer. Joe raised his
hand as if to strike Paul.

"Two," Paul whispered.

"Where are they?"

Paul looked confused. Joe refined his question.
"Where in the house are they?"

"You promise you won't kill me?"

"Yes."

Paul hesitated. Not out of cunning, just fear. Joe
raised his hand again. Paul spoke quickly, half-gasping:
"There's one guy on the first floor, in the kitchen,
with the cameras, and one guy on the second floor. He
sits in the hallway."

Joe figured that there were plenty of cameras for

security reasons, as well as cameras in the fucking rooms. Blackmail was another good source of revenue. He took out the picture of Lisa. He hit the overhead light and held the snapshot in front of Paul's face. "Do they have a playground? Is this girl inside?"

A new fear crossed Paul's face. He looked to his left and right. He wanted out. Joe turned off the light and crushed Paul's windpipe, then let go. "Is the girl in the picture inside?"

Paul nodded and whispered, "Yes." He was scared and ashamed. He wasn't a hard case, and he gave Joe everything he needed. Joe removed the key to the brownstone from Paul's sweatshirt pocket, and he got the basic layout of the house and the operation from him—the booker-madam worked off-premises, there was no landline, only cell phones, and the greeting lounge was on the first floor; there were six bedrooms altogether, on the second and third floors; the playground was on the third floor, last bedroom at the end of the hall, and in the bedroom next to Lisa's was her "big sister."

The "big sister" was usually a prostitute in her early thirties, who, trying to hang on near the end of her career, makes herself useful by chaperoning and befriending the young ones—training them, shopping for them, and feeding them a steady diet of Vicodin, Klonopin, Xanax, and Oxycontin, all of which kept the girls on the playground pliant and docile. Paul, who was addicted to painkillers, often bought his own pills from Lisa's chaperone, which was one more way for the big sister to turn a profit for herself before she was sent to the street, no longer of value, but at least, unlike the children, there was no need to kill her when she was used up.

Joe, having gotten all the information he wanted, closed his hand once more around Paul's throat and the carotid artery that led to his brain. Paul's eyes widened at the betrayal, and Joe counted to ten. Those ten seconds seemed rubbery and strange to Joe. Looking at Paul's face, he had a vision of sorts. He saw Paul entering a bar, catching his reflection in the glass of the door, and quickly running his fingers through his hair, since he never liked how he looked, and how Paul felt in that moment, without being able to put words to it, that everything in his life seemed to fall short.

Then Paul was asleep, not dead, and Joe lowered him down gently across the backseat, checking his pulse and his breathing. He smoothed Paul's hair, as Paul had in the vision, and, like a god, he looked at Paul with tenderness. He imagined Paul's little apartment somewhere, his mean, unmade bed, his private place where he worried over himself, where he went to hide like an animal. Joe knew that all human beings are the star of their own very important film, a film in which they are both camera and actor; a film in which they are always playing the fearful and lonely hero who gets up each day hoping to finally strike upon the life they are meant to lead, though they never do.

He then taped Paul's head and neck to the seat and put tape over his mouth, cutting a little slit for breathing. He bent Paul's knees and taped his legs—his heels to the backs of his thighs—like he was roping a piece of cattle. He didn't want Paul to wake up and make a fuss, kicking at the window. Then Joe got out of the car. It was time to get the girl.

He came through the front door of the brothel as the guard from the kitchen came into the hall, having seen Joe on the monitor. He didn't reach for his gun, which was a mistake. He was big, six-five, a linebacker's body. He was about twenty feet from Joe.

"Who the fuck are you?" he asked. His meaty head was shaved. It was gleaming and ugly.

Joe sprinted at him, the hammer raised. The guard, scared by the hammer and scared by Joe, fumbled for his gun, and Joe was on him. The hammer struck him on the cheek, on the neck, and in the center of his back, where he felt it deep in his lungs as he went down.

Joe then kicked him on the side of his pink, razor-nicked head. Joe was good at damaging people without killing them. He had been in the house less than ten seconds.

The stairway was to his right. He took it two steps at a time, and the second guard, a squat and powerfully built black man, appeared at the top of the stairs, mystified by the noises that had come from below. Joe came right at him with the hammer, backing him up, and hit him on his collarbone, snapping it. The guard stumbled back into the hallway, and Joe, swinging the hammer like a baseball bat, sent it into the man's breastplate, and he went down. Joe kicked him in the head and he was out.

Then a john, in pants but no shirt, emerged from the bedroom closest to the fallen guard, and Joe hit him in the shoulder with the hammer, crumpling him. Then he kicked him hard in the stomach to keep him quiet for a while. The man, like a bug trying to swim, scratched at the floor in agony.

No one else emerged from the second-floor bedrooms, so Joe took the stairs to the third floor. He wasn't worried about any of the johns or the prostitutes making cell-phone calls. At all times, even when not working, Joe carried a jammer in his pocket. They were cheap, only 150 dollars, and blocked cell-phone reception in a twenty-yard radius. He had started using them when he moved back in with his mother. He liked to ride the bus sometimes on Queens Boulevard and stare out the window, but he couldn't stand listening to everyone on their phones.

He went to the playground, per Paul's instructions, and opened the door. In the glow from the hallway, he saw a man's back, like an enormous white tumor. It was grotesque—arched and pistoning. He could make out the girl's ankles on either side of the man's fatty white thighs, but that was all he could see of her.

The man turned, looked at Joe, his eyes full of rage—how dare he be disturbed, he was paying good money for this—and Joe struck him in the face with the hammer, knocking him off the girl and sending him sprawling. Joe then grabbed the man by the arm, tossed him to the floor, and sent his steel-toed boot into his testicles, exploding them. Then he kicked him in the head to stop his screams.

The girl was lying inert on the bed, her head to the side, her lips moving. Her legs were still open. She looked like a torn-apart doll. Joe leaned his face close to hers to make a positive ID, and to hear what she was whispering. It was barely audible, but she was counting. She was in the seven hundreds. Her eyes were open but glazed. Then her big sister, a skinny diet-pill blonde with artificial tits, wearing a silk robe, came into the room. She saw the bloody, unconscious man on the floor, his groin looking like an animal that's been skinned.

"What's going on?" she asked, inanely, hysterically. Joe, seeing that she carried no weapon, advanced on her, grabbed her elbow violently, and said, "Get her dressed. *Fast.*" He saw clothing on a chair—a Catholic schoolgirl's outfit, a tawdry cliché.

The big sister was in shock, but she got the girl out of bed and into her skirt and blouse and panties, not bothering with the white stockings or little black shoes. Joe took a sheet from the bed, wrapped the girl in it, and carried her past the men he had left on the ground, down the two flights of stairs, and out of the brothel.

At the top of the stoop, he peered up and down the street. No cop cars. With the girl light in his arms, he moved quickly to his rental. About six minutes had passed since Joe had gone in. He put the girl in the front seat. She was out of it but not completely.

He dragged Paul out of the car and left him on the sidewalk. He dropped the bloody hammer in a sewer, started the car, and headed for the W Hotel. He glanced at the girl. Her face was against the window. Her lips were moving. She was still counting. *It's her way to get through it*, Joe thought. *She counts until it's over.*

———

Joe left the car in front of the W, told the doorman he'd be right back and gave him a twenty. He carried Lisa, in the sheet, across the lobby and to the front desk. She rested her head on his shoulder, asleep now like a child who's been on a long car ride and is being carried to her bed. She felt precious to Joe, fragile like a bird. He hoped that Votto, without his wife, could look after her.

The lone, sleek-looking clerk at the front desk hid his discomfort at the sight of the tall man carrying a child wrapped in a sheet. It was hard to know what to make of it, something was strange—the man was wearing latex gloves—but he knew to stay cool. That's what they teach you at Cornell's hotel school, especially if you're going to work the after-midnight shift in a city hotel.

"Senator Votto," Joe said. "He's expecting me. Tell him it's Joe."

The clerk nodded, picked up the desk phone, dialed the room, and waited. Then: "There's someone here named Joe, sir. Send him up?" He nodded silently to whatever was said on the other end, hung up the phone, and came around the desk, leading Joe to the elevators, his hips swaying like a woman's. There was an elevator ready, and the clerk swiped his card inside, freeing the system. As Joe carried Lisa past him into the elevator, he smelled the man's cloying perfume, and then hit the tenth-floor button.

He carried her down the hall to Votto's room, and the door was slightly open. Joe pushed it in with his foot and stepped inside, and three uniformed cops with guns raised—one of which was equipped with a silencer—came at Joe from his right and his left. Two from the bedroom and one from the living room. Votto wasn't there. The cops seemed out of breath, nervous and hurried, as if they had just arrived. They closed the door behind him.

"Move," said the alpha of the three, a beefy Irish-looking cop in his mid-thirties, with red splotches on both his cheeks. His gun had the silencer, and he waved it, indicating that Joe should carry the girl into the living room, where he'd sat with Votto hours before. They were in the narrow entry space by the front door, and the cop wanted room. Joe couldn't risk the girl getting shot, so he did what he was told. The other two cops then relieved him of the girl and carried her back out of the suite. She was still asleep, drugged, in shock. Joe heard the door to the outer hallway close. Where were they taking her? Where was Votto? The alpha cop kept his gun on Joe. They hadn't frisked him for weapons, but all he had was the cutting razor.

"Sit down, asshole," the cop said, "keep your hands in front of you." He took out his cell phone with his left hand, hit a button with his thumb. Joe sat down. He cursed himself. He had turned his jammer off when he drove to the W, wanting to conserve the

battery. The television in the living room was on—
NY1, the twenty-four-hour local news station, was
playing. The cop, still standing, kept his eyes and the
gun on Joe. It was a .22, good for a close-range pop to
the head. Assassins prefer to use a .22: its ballistics are
nearly impossible to trace.

The cop held the phone to his ear, waiting. The
coffee table was between them. It had a despoiled
room-service tray on it: a meal had been eaten. Several
empty mini-bottles of liquor were also on the table, as
well as two empty bottles of red wine. Votto or someone had been doing a fair amount of sloppy drinking.

"I have him," the cop said into the phone. "What
do you want—"

That was when Joe propelled himself across the
cluttered table and into the cop's legs, but the table
kept Joe from going as far as he would have liked.
He hit the cop's knees, backing him up, causing him
to drop the cell phone, but he didn't knock the cop
down, as he had hoped.

Like trying to run in a dream, Joe felt himself to be
moving in slow motion, pulling himself up the cop's
body, his left hand all the while on the cop's wrist
that controlled the gun, and the cop was trying to
free the gun, to get the right angle, and he was chop-
ping at the back of Joe's head with the butt of it, land-
ing sharp blows, and then the cop got the gun loose

and, trying to shoot Joe in the back as Joe still clawed upward, shot him in the calf, and it felt like a welding torch had burned a hole through his right leg, but Joe kept climbing and climbing. He was blind, danger was like that sometimes, your eyes stopped working, some unseeing snake part of your brain took over, where everything was shadow and feeling, and Joe again had his left hand on the wrist that held the gun, and he was pushing it away, a shot was fired into the wall, and Joe was standing up now, his momentum driving them into the desk.

He thought he had been moving slowly, but he had actually been moving very quickly, and he could feel the cop's great animal strength and will to live pushing back against his own, and they went down to the floor and rolled, and Joe came up on top, his body flat against the cop's like they were lovers, and he still had the shooting hand under his control, and the cop was pounding at him with his left fist and thrashing and kicking his legs. He was a wild, large, gross thing beneath Joe, his breath warm and rancid with fear and rage, and then Joe got his hand under the cop's chin and with all his strength he pushed the cop's head back unnaturally until the neck snapped, and the whole thing beneath him shuddered, a tremor that ran from head to toe—Joe felt it like a wave beneath him, like a blanket being fanned out over a bed—until all the life was gone and the thing that had been a cop, a man, went still.

Joe rolled off, panting, his vision returning. He scrambled to his feet, his right calf felt ballooned and on fire and was bleeding profusely, but he didn't have time to mess with the wound. He had no choice but to leave a blood spoor. He took the cop's .22 and, dragging his wounded leg, he went quickly down the hall toward the emergency staircase, which he couldn't access from the lobby earlier in the day. No hotel guests came out of their rooms. The silencer had worked.

Joe pushed open the metal door and flung himself down the gray-painted staircase, swinging his bad leg as fast as he could. He had the gun in his hand—he expected a cop or someone to emerge at each floor—but they weren't on to him yet. He was angry at himself for not taking the cop's cell phone to figure out who he was talking to, but it was too late for that, and anyway a cell phone was like a tracking device and Joe had to get in the clear.

He made it to the parking garage in the basement. No one was there. He moved as quickly as he could up the ramp, until he came to the lot's exit on Carlisle Street, which was on the other side of the hotel. He couldn't risk circling the block and getting his rental car, which was on Washington Street at the front of the W. Whoever the cop had been talking to would have somebody there very soon, maybe the same cops who had taken the girl. So he limped rapidly up to Greenwich Street, holding the gun in his pocket. A little bit of luck was on his side: a taxi was heading downtown, and Joe hailed it, got into the car, looked through the back window—no one was coming.

"Coney Island, Surf Avenue, in front of the stadium," Joe said. "I'll give you a nice tip for going to Brooklyn."

The driver grunted, displeased, and headed for the Brooklyn Battery Tunnel. Joe's leg needed attention, but he didn't want to go to a Manhattan hospital. He'd go to Coney Island Hospital, though he didn't want the driver to know that and be able to tell someone later. He had left blood in the hotel room and on the stairwell, and pretty soon they would be looking for a wounded man fitting Joe's description. They'd start with the hospitals that were closest to the hotel. So Coney Island, miles away, was a good choice.

Also, McCleary lived near the water, right by Kingsborough College, not far from the hospital, and Joe's instinct as a Marine, when a mission goes bad, was to report to his commanding officer, and in this case that was McCleary, and this was a mission that had certainly gone bad. Dirty cops were involved, and Joe had just killed one of them. He took the duct tape out of his pocket and, using the cutting razor, made a tourniquet for himself. He didn't want to lose his leg from the knee down. He was acquiring enemies— enemies he didn't know—and he needed to be whole.

Joe went to an all-night bodega on Surf Avenue and bought a quart bottle of Budweiser and a small bottle of rubbing alcohol, which was next to the condoms and the toothpaste. Then he went out to the beach, limping across the sand, and sat near the water so that his screams wouldn't be heard by the few late-night stragglers walking like zombies up and down the boardwalk against the cold wind.

A three-quarters moon had come out, just enough light for Joe to see by. He cut the tape off and rolled up his pant leg. The wound started to bleed. The bullet had torn a gutter through his calf muscle, but it could have been much worse. If it had hit the bone or his Achilles tendon, he'd be in bad shape. He tilted the bottle back and gulped from the beer. He wanted to reek of beer in the emergency room to help his cover story ring true—he had been drinking, decided to do a little late-night home-repair work, and had shot himself with his nail gun. His construction-worker appearance would also help to sell the story.

Then he put on a fresh pair of latex gloves, poured the rubbing alcohol on his razor and on the gash, and, not suppressing his screams, he peeled back the skin of his calf, like opening the flap of an envelope. He dug around inside the wound with his fingers and the sharp blade, making a mess of the thing. The thin ropes of his flesh felt like a pod of small snakes.

After nearly a minute, the pain became too much and, needing to stop, Joe quit damaging himself and let loose one more doglike howl. Then he was quiet, almost peaceful. He stared at the water, one or two ships blinked far away on the horizon, like fallen planets, and the ocean was a rolling black tongue, content for the time being to just taste the land. Joe looked back down at his ripped-open leg. He hoped it would pass inspection. He didn't want the doctor to look too closely and see that it was a bullet wound and put in a call to the local precinct, which would be standard procedure.

He cut up his pant leg to obscure the tear made by the bullet's entrance and exit, then lowered the shredded fabric and wrapped a lot of fresh tape around it, making a new tourniquet, which would add to his do-it-yourself, drinking-man story. He finished the beer, tried to lessen the burning pain in his calf with steady breathing, and replayed in his mind the scene at the hotel.

Nothing added up. Whoever operated the brothel must have known who the girl was, but how would

they know Votto was in town? How would they
know where Joe was taking her? And how high up the
food chain did this go? If you run a brothel, no matter
how much it brings in, you don't have dirty cops who
carry silencers on your speed dial. You have cops but
not cops who are assassins. Someone very high up had
been contacted and made that call. There hadn't been
time to get private killers. They called the badged
killers who were already on the street, on duty, ready
to go. Joe had left the brothel at approximately 1:30
and gotten to the W about fifteen minutes later. The
cops seemed like they had arrived just before he did.

And where was Votto? Was he in danger or somehow involved? If he was involved, it made no sense.
Why wouldn't he be there to see his daughter? Why
would he try to have Joe killed? And where was the
girl now? Votto, if he was alive, would have answers,
but he needed McCleary to get to Votto. He dragged
himself back out to Surf, found a working pay phone,
and called McCleary's cell. It went right to voice
mail. He tried the old man's landline and it went to a
phone-company digital voice mail. Joe hoped the old
man was asleep, that he turned his ringers off at night.

He didn't like to leave a message, but if they had
Votto, they might get to McCleary. He said: "Be careful. Things are bad." Then he called the cell again
and left the same message. McCleary was old, but he

was tough. He could handle himself. Joe limped a few blocks to the hospital, and he started to enjoy the pain, thinking of it as a punishment for his failures.

In the unclean, ugly-bright Coney Island Hospital emergency room, Joe, after signing in, had to wait. A stabbing victim and a car accident with three injured parties had shown up just before him, it was a busy night, and his tape-job, for the time being, was keeping his leg together. So he waited to be attended to, tried to get comfortable in the plastic bucket seat, and after he had been there about twenty minutes, something happened that caught his attention.

A television hanging in the corner, suspended by chains like a television in a prison ward, was playing loudly, bothering Joe, but it was tuned to NY1. It was a channel he never watched with his mother, but now twice in one night he was aware of it, and a news segment from earlier in the evening was being rebroadcast. A man had jumped from the Sheraton in Midtown around 10:30 p.m. The reporter was on the scene. The body had landed on a parked taxi, but on the passenger side. Two feet over and the driver would have been dead. They showed the caved-in taxi, though the body had been removed.

Then the driver was being interviewed. That

would have been enough to make it newsworthy—
the taxi driver's narrow escape—but this was an
extra-special suicide. The man who had jumped was
a state senator from Albany named Stephen Wilson.
Joe wondered if State Senator Votto knew State Senator Wilson. He figured he must, and he wondered if
Votto's disappearing act tonight was somehow linked
to the suicide. It seemed like too much of a coinci-
dence. Something was going down.

Then his name was called. His story worked on
the exhausted ER doctor, and forty-five stitches and
three hours later, Joe was released. He tried McCleary's
numbers from a hospital pay phone, but everything
went straight to voice mail. Joe didn't leave any messages this time. It was nearly six a.m. He figured there
was a good chance McCleary was still asleep. He
hoped he was still asleep.

Taped to the pay phone was a card for a car service, which he called. As the sun came up, he was
driven over to McCleary's dead-end street. It ran along-
side a little harbor and waterway that fed into the
Atlantic. Some of the houses were gaudy and cheap,
but it was a beautiful spot. He had the driver go past
McCleary's house, a simple, white-brick two-story
affair with a living-room window that had a view of
the ocean. McCleary's ten-year-old Caddy was in the
narrow driveway. Joe got dropped off at the end of

tried the knob—it was unlocked, as it usually was when McCleary was working. So Joe opened the door and something was blocking it. He pushed against whatever it was and squeezed in. It was McCleary blocking the door. He was facedown on the floor, the back of his head shot off, like a hairpiece had been removed. He had been kneeling and was shot execution style.

Joe stared at the large pool of blood around the head. Some of it was starting to dry, turning brown like mud, wanting to clot even now. He figured McCleary had been dead maybe two hours. Joe squatted down, put on a fresh pair of latex gloves, and reached under the body. He searched McCleary's jacket and pants pockets. His wallet and cell phone were gone, and the laptop on his desk was gone. It was meant to look like a robbery.

Joe stood up and glanced around the tiny office, his eyes scanning—the file-cabinet drawers were open, more stage setting—and he flashed to McCleary behind his desk, smoking a cigarette, acting tough. It was almost like he was alive again, which was a better way to leave things. So, not looking back down at the body, he went to step out, wiped the door handle with his T-shirt, and then stepped back in fast. Something had bothered him: McCleary's Rolodex was missing.

He went behind the desk, looked on the floor.

the street, which was at the water's edge. The driver did a U-turn and left.

Joe looked around. He didn't see anything that looked out of place. There was no overnight parking on the street, so the only cars were the ones in drive-ways and, ostensibly, they would be the homeowners' cars. Joe couldn't be certain, but he didn't think McCleary had visitors. Everything felt calm. Nobody was up yet. He walked toward McCleary's house.

Sailboats at the other end of the waterway, in the little harbor, were moored, rocking peacefully, clink-ing, like wind chimes. *McCleary has done all right*, Joe thought. He had never been here before, but he had memorized the address when he first started working with McCleary just in case he ever had to come here, just in case things went bad.

McCleary had bought this place on the water thinking it would be his wife's reward for all the years they had lived on a trooper's salary. But she was only in the house for three months when she died, breaking McCleary in half, though he hadn't yet followed her to the grave the way a lot of longtime spouses do— one dies and the other is quick to join.

Joe took the gun out, shielding it from view, and limped up the three steps to the front door. He pushed the bell. Waited. Nothing. When McCleary didn't answer after a third ring, Joe put his hand through the

Looked all over. There was no Rolodex. McCleary, under duress, must have given him up. Joe knew what this meant. From Angel's phone number in the bodega—a landline number—they could get Angel's address. Why hadn't he insisted that McCleary rip up the number right in front of him? *Because I'm fucking slipping,* Joe thought. *It started in Cincinnati.*

Joe's eyes blacked over, like a hood had been draped over his head, and there was a shriek of terror in his mind, something he hadn't felt in years. Then he willed the terror away and willed himself to see. He called information from McCleary's office phone and got the bodega's number. He let it ring and ring, but nobody answered. This was not a good sign. Angel lived above the bodega and opened up by six a.m. each day of the week. Joe didn't have Angel's cellphone number, and Angel, like most people, didn't have a landline in his residence, so Joe couldn't call him there on the off chance that he was upstairs and not working for some reason. There was simply no way to warn him, if it was even still possible.

And if they got to Angel, they could get to his mother because of Moises, and there was no way to warn her, either. They had a landline, but the ringer was always off because the only calls they got were from telemarketers. People from her church used to call, but that had stopped a while back. But even if he could reach his mother, she hadn't been out of the house in years. She wasn't capable anymore, she couldn't walk that well—he did all the shopping. And he had never spoken to any of the neighbors, couldn't get someone to help her. His paranoia, previously a safeguard, a protective wall, was now a liability.

He called the fire department in Rego Park, told them smoke was coming from his mother's address, then hung up. He didn't want to call cops to the house, he didn't know the reach of the people he was up against, but maybe the fire department might get there at just the right time. Might scare off his pursuers for a little while, let him get home and get his mother out of there. It was a long shot, but he had to take it.

Then Joe left the building. Using a credit card, the same one that he had used at the hospital, he went to an ATM and got more cash. He had two identifications left, having burned the one attached to the rental car. He got a taxi and gave the driver Angel's address. He still couldn't risk being down in the subway. But it was rush hour now, and the ride from Manhattan to Queens would take a while.

The driver headed for the Midtown Tunnel, and Joe's only hope was that McCleary's killers had gotten to the bodega *after* Moises went to school. That would slow them down. They were looking for him and he was looking for them, but they were in the lead. There was the chance, too, that they hadn't yet gotten to the bodega at all, maybe Angel's phone was down or there was some other explanation for him not answering. So he had to go there first, and the bodega was on his way to his mother. If Angel was there, he would give him money, tell him to take Moises out of the city and lay low for a while. He knew that Angel's wife worked as a nurse at a hospice in Rockland County and came home on the weekends. They could go to her. If it wasn't too late.

He stared out at the sluggish traffic. There was nothing he could do to move more quickly. He had to accept this. He thought about McCleary on the floor, and he thought about the girl, her face pressed to the window, counting. He thought about his mother opening the door to police officers. Why wouldn't she? Then he closed his eyes and elevated his leg on the seat. *I need to sleep*, he thought. *I need to do better.*

It took them forty agonizing minutes to get to Queens. Joe had the taxi wait, but the bodega was closed.

Joe then had the taxi drop him off four blocks from his mother's house. He began a methodical sweep of the streets leading up to the house, peering into each parked vehicle. He was looking for an unmarked police car. He didn't think they'd leave a standard cruiser on the street for him to see. After looking into sixty-three cars, he found it two blocks from his mother's house, a black Dodge Charger. The dashboard emergency beacon, which they used when they broke cover, was on the front seat, the telltale sign of an unmarked cruiser. The presence of the Dodge confirmed to Joe that they were inside. His call to the fire department had most likely achieved nothing. They had probably swung by the house and registered it as a false alarm.

He then circled the long way around and entered the wide alleyway behind the strip of houses where he had grown up. Three houses from his mother's, he climbed on top of the shed of one of his neighbors. His leg was giving him trouble, but he made up for it with arm strength. From the shed he was able to get hold of a fire escape, which he took all the way to the roof. A few years ago, he had noticed this shed, its proximity to the fire escape, and had filed away the information.

All the roofs of the houses were on the same level, and the houses were all joined, a late-1940s postwar Rego Park construction style that was to Joe's bene-fit. His bad leg couldn't support much weight, but the roofs were not at a severe angle, so he was able to traverse them fairly easily. The houses were only two stories high, and the trees in the backyards, which were still holding on to half of their foliage, were giv-ing good cover. There was a slight breeze in the air, and the trees seemed to be talking to each other, their language the hush of the trembling leaves.

From his own roof he was able to lower himself onto the fire escape outside his mother's bedroom window, which she always kept open a crack, believing in fresh air for health, as well as the superstition that an open window kept malicious spirits from staying inside, from feeling trapped. He gently and quietly removed the screen, placing it on the fire escape, and then he pushed the window up, soundlessly. He could see his mother's form on the bed, a pillow over her head.

He entered the room. Moises and Angel were on the floor, fallen over like chess pieces, the backs of their skulls shot off. For his mother, they had held a pillow over her face and then shot her that way, not being able to look at an old lady as they took her out. *They're weak*, he thought.

He heard them downstairs, whispering quietly. They weren't expecting him to come from above. There were two of them, and he knew exactly where they were just from the sounds of their voices. The house was like an extension of his nervous system, his skin. He had spent the first thirteen years of his life listening for the slightest movement of his father, ready to run and hide if something didn't sound right. He could tell by the way his father closed the refrigerator door or the way his foot landed on the staircase if something bad was going to happen, so if he hid quickly, he might escape a beating. He always had a few spots, which he often changed and rotated, where his father couldn't find him.

The sin of it, though, was that when he hid well, he knew his mother was usually the second choice. Many times, barely breathing, tucked away at the bottom of a laundry hamper or on the shelf of a closet, all his limbs dead and cramped, he listened while she cried, feeling a terrible selfish relief that it wasn't him. As he got older, around age nine, he knew that God could never forgive him this selfishness, this sin.

He lifted the scorched pillow off her face. *I've never been able to protect her,* he thought. Her face was destroyed. The bullet had passed through the left eye. Something happened inside his mind. It was physical. He could feel it in the center of his brain—it was as if large plate-glass windows were breaking, one after the other. When the noise stopped—he didn't know how long it lasted—he cocked his head. They were still whispering. One was hiding by the front door, the other by the kitchen door.

The staircase from the second floor to the living room was only five steps. If he had two good legs, he could jump down the steps all at once and take out the one by the front door. After that, it would be best-man-wins between him and the one in the kitchen. But he had only one good leg.

He put the pillow back over his mother's face. He walked very quietly to her door, glancing at Angel and his son. He was glad they were facedown, that he didn't have to meet their eyes. From his mother's door to the top of the staircase was just a few feet. He crossed them without noise.

He figured that when he jumped his leg would buckle—there was no way around it—so he had to factor that into his shooting. He took out the .22. There were nine bullets left in the clip. He didn't want the neighbors to hear anything. McCleary's .45, which would be much louder, was the backup.

He leaped down the stairs, his leg crumpling as he expected—in a flash he saw the shocked face of the undercover cop by the front door—and he did a roll, came up with the .22, and shot the cop once in the heart and once in the mouth. Joe was facing away from the kitchen as he squeezed the second shot, and the other one came running into the living room—also equipped with a silenced .22, their weapon of choice—and shot rapidly at Joe, firing off three shots, all of them high. Joe was rolling on the floor, trying to turn, to face the cop, and then the cop's gun jammed, making things easy. Joe shot him in the throat and he dropped. He bled out very quickly. Both men were dead.

He took out their phones—they were communi-
cating with their superiors by text. This made things
simpler. He could masquerade as them for a little while,
which would give him some time, but he wanted to
move quickly, very quickly.

He lived in a very minimal way—he had only one
valise's worth of clothing. Most important, because he
was going to need a new look, he had a nice dark blue
suit and a yellow tie that he had used for church the
first few years he had been at home—his mother had
still gone to Sunday Mass then. Other than his meager
amount of clothing, including one good pair of shoes,
he had no personal effects, except for a briefcase, which
had his passports and the banking information for
his different aliases. He filled a small toilet bag with his
shaving needs and added that to the suitcase. Though
he had all his possessions, his instinct was to leave
absolutely no trace of himself, no DNA-rich evidence.
He thought of burning the house down, but he didn't
want to risk killing any neighbors. The house would
have to be left intact.

While he finished packing, a text came in on
the first cop's phone: "Anything?" He looked at the
cop's style in his earlier responses. "All quiet," he
texted back.

He then found the keys to the unmarked car on the
body of the one he had shot in the throat. He limped
to the car as fast as he could and double-parked it in

front of the house, its hazard lights blinking. From the basement he got two large black garbage bags and, doubling them up, put his mother inside.

From her bedroom, he carried her down to the living room and looked out the window of the front door. Nobody was on the street. He then quickly brought her out to the car, placing her gently on the backseat. He didn't want strangers touching her body when they came to the house. There was nothing he could do for Angel and Moises.

He wrote down what seemed to be the important names and numbers from the cops' phones—their most recent calls and texts—and then left the phones with the bodies so he couldn't be tracked. He took their weapons—they both had silenced .22s, as well as Glocks, with regular barrels, in their ankle holsters. He took their extra ammunition clips. He wouldn't have to buy any black-market guns or ammo for a little while, but for what he had planned, he would need to eventually.

He drove the unmarked car out of Queens and across the Fifty-ninth Street Bridge. He took the Harlem River Drive north to the lower level of the George Washington and crossed into New Jersey. It was late morning now, and off the Palisades Parkway, about five miles from the bridge, he pulled into a parking lot, which had a scenic view of the Hudson from the high cliffs of the Palisades.

There was a dirt path you could walk along to a higher promontory, hidden by trees, for an even more spectacular view of the river, the bridge, and Manhattan. It was a clear, cold day, and the world looked magnificent—the make-believe city and the ancient river.

He got out of the car and went on the path, carrying his mother in the doubled-up garbage bags—she didn't weigh much in life or death. There were no tourists about, and he added a very large rock to the sack and then sealed it tight with the duct tape. When he got to the promontory, he tossed her with all his might into the water hundreds of feet below. No one saw. He watched her make a dimple in the water, float a moment, and then sink. It was the most beautiful funeral he could think to give her.

Then he drove to a gas station off the Palisades, which had a parking lot for commuters to catch buses into the city. He didn't want to hold on to the car much longer. They would be tracking it soon. He called a Fort Lee taxi to come pick him up. He had the taxi take him to a motel off Route 4, near the bridge.

He checked into a room, shaved his head, showered, keeping his leg dry, and then put on his suit. He was now a bald businessman, carrying a suitcase and a briefcase. They were looking for a construction worker in a black baseball hat.

The shower was a meager substitute for sleep, but he was grateful for it, and he made some instant coffee that came with the room. It was more of a placebo than anything else. He was running on adrenaline. The hunt had begun.

With his credit card, he used the hotel phone to call information in Albany. After two attempts, he was put through to Senator Votto's office. A receptionist answered. Joe did his best to come across as a half-cocked citizen. When he wanted, Joe could play many characters, do many voices. He was a great mimic, a great liar.

"I voted for Senator Votto," Joe said to the receptionist in a self-important rush. "Can I come in and talk to him? The cops in my town are giving out too many tickets. I got one for a dirty license plate. This is taxation, not law enforcement. It's not fair. He should do something about this."

"Senator Votto meets with constituents every Friday, from nine to twelve. This Friday is all booked, but you can make an appointment for next week."

"Will he definitely be in this Friday?" Joe asked. "I could just show up and if somebody misses their appointment, he could see me, like when you go to the doctor."

"I wouldn't suggest that. What's your name? We can put you down for next week."

Joe cut her off. "Will he be in *this* Friday? I don't want to pay this ticket."

"Yes, but—"

Joe hung up the phone. He had the information he needed. Votto was alive. He then called another taxi and had it take him to Macy's on Thirty-fourth Street, back in the city. He picked up a tan raincoat to wear over his suit. Then, favoring his bad leg, he walked a block to Penn Station and bought a train ticket to Albany. He only had to wait forty-five minutes. He wasn't experiencing hunger, but he got a container of soup. In the Marines you ate whenever you could, no matter what was happening. He bought all three newspapers and got some reading glasses. They added to his cover. He sat on a bench and read the papers. There was an article about the suicide of Senator Wilson in the late edition of the *Post*.

Wilson was a married father of three who had recently separated from his wife. Unspecified drugs were found in his hotel room. He had jumped from the roof. The article implied that a suicide note had been left—foul play was not suspected.

Joe got on the train to Albany and stared out the window. He was going to find out for sure—he figured he had some things wrong—but he thought it had all gone down something like this:

Votto runs for office. The name recognition gets him in

and also the story of redemption—he will undo his father's legacy of corruption. And he probably believes it himself, thinks he'll be clean, not like his dad. Then the men who had run his father for thirty-five years begin to threaten him, want a piece of him. Albany spends twenty-five billion dollars a year on construction and road building. It's a bigger racket than drugs, gambling, or prostitution. So they need a man in Albany, and Votto is it. He will be their new boy or one of their new boys. But, not wanting to be like his father, he resists, and so they punish him.

They abduct his daughter, put her to work as a whore, and say they'll kill her if he doesn't do what they want, and if he tries to report them, he and his wife will be killed. He's weak, doesn't know how to fight back. They promise him they'll let his daughter go in a year if he shows himself to be loyal. So he lets everyone believe the Facebook story that the mob cooked up—they even came up with a phony computer trail for the cops to find. His wife figures out that Votto is somehow complicit, but he tells her there's nothing they can do. Despairing, she kills herself.

So Votto sits on all of this for six months. It's a living hell, but he survives. He sometimes thinks of how his daughter loathed him, and this makes it a little easier.

Then he gets that text, it's rubbed in his face what's been done to him and his family, and he cracks. He comes down to New York and calls McCleary. Fuck the mob, he's going to get his daughter back, and he's going to kill the bastard who raped her. It was too much to bear that someone he must have known had violated her. But he can't involve the cops, because they might figure out what really happened.

So Joe takes the job. While Joe is sitting in his car on Forty-eighth Street, Votto is getting drunk at the W. To distract himself, he puts on the TV. NY1 comes on. He sees that Stephen Wilson has killed himself. He knows Wilson. He knows he has demons. He knows in his gut that it was Wilson who texted him. The text was Wilson's confession, his last. Votto sits there in the W. What has he done? His anger dissipates. Wilson's death resets everything back to the way it was. The mob will kill him and his daughter for pulling this stunt, for hiring McCleary and Joe.

He can't think straight. Then he decides. He'll call them, explain what's happened. They'll have to understand. How much can a man take? But at least he came to his senses— he warned them—and they'll be ready for Joe, keep him from getting his daughter.

But by the time Votto calls, Joe is already heading for the W. The girl is leaning her head against the passenger window. While Votto is talking to them, pleading, explaining, the security guards at the brothel come to and make their calls. So now Votto's handlers have to scramble. They tell Votto to get out of the hotel. They have dirty cops ready on an as-needed basis. They send them to the W to intercept Joe.

They figure they'll kill Joe and put everything back the way it was. They want to keep Votto working for them. He's more valuable than his daughter, but she's their control over him. But Joe kills the cop. This complicates things. They need everything clean. They've got to protect their asset, their politician. They can't have people like Joe running around, people who know something, even if what they know is just a thread.

From Votto they get McCleary. McCleary will give them Joe. They probably pick him up around 4:30 in the morning. He had been asleep when Joe first called, but while Joe is getting stitched up, they go right to McCleary's house, ring his bell. They wake McCleary and he answers the door. Doesn't take his gun. He's tired. He's old. They put pressure on him. They want Joe. He says the only link to Joe is back at his office. They take him there. He gives them the Rolodex. They shoot him in the head. They go to the bodega. They learn where Joe lives.

Angel, Moises, and Joe's mother are now just pieces of garbage in the way and can't be left out there. They want this thing very clean. Access to twenty-five billion Albany dollars makes this imperative. So they need to find Joe and eliminate him. They check all the hospitals, and they have the two undercover cops waiting at his house. They should have sent more.

Now Joe is on a train to Albany, and he has phone numbers to work with. But his first step is to find Votto, see how much of the story he's got right. He figures he has it pretty close, but he can't be certain, and he wants all the facts. And from Votto he'll find out where the girl has been taken, get her to safety, and finish the job.

Then he'll wage a slow war, working his way up the food chain until he gets to the man who pulled the trigger on all of this. Joe wants to bleed him. First he'll kill everyone beneath him and let him feel Joe coming for a while. He'll also go after his sons, if he has any, pick them off one by one. After that, he'll kidnap the bastard, take him somewhere, and cut him to pieces over a few weeks, always stitching him back up, keeping him alive. But each day, methodically, he'll remove his fingers, toes, feet, hands, testicles, penis, tongue, nose.

Then maybe at the end he won't kill him. He'll leave him that way. Drop him off at a hospital. Let him survive. A limbless, deformed creature. The man who killed McCleary, Angel, and Moises. The man who killed his mother. The man who told someone to pull a trigger.

These were the things Joe thought about as he looked out the window of his train. The Hudson, to the left of the tracks, was impossibly beautiful, a blue darker than the sky, and for long stretches, the riverbanks, thick with forest, were free of modern blight. One could almost imagine that this was how the river had been for thousands of years.

But Joe saw none of this. He only looked inward, plotting. At his core, Joe was a very angry boy who had never gotten proper vengeance on his father, which is what a boy like Joe needed. Though it's not always vengeance; sometimes it's justice.

When he arrived in Albany a little after four p.m., Joe took a cab to the Hilton, which was three blocks from the grotesque and hideous capitol building. A nineteenth-century Romanesque monstrosity made of stone and with numerous pointed gables, the capitol looked more like a castle than a seat of government.

Joe chose the Hilton because an expensive hotel was better cover, and it matched his appearance—his suit and raincoat. If they thought he might come to Albany looking for Votto, they wouldn't think to put a man at the Hilton.

He took a room with a view of the parking lot, which was all that was available. He told the girl behind the reception desk, who seemed genuinely concerned, that it wasn't a problem. He was not in Albany to be a tourist.

Transaction at the desk completed, he limped to the elevator bank. A businessman in a raincoat would not take the stairs. Like the beginning of a parable, he said to himself, "A man with one leg has nowhere to run." But he had no idea where that came from or why he thought it. And he wasn't sure it was true. The elevator opened and he disappeared inside.

After putting his suitcase and briefcase in his room, Joe went to the business center. Sitting at one of the bulky computers that were hardly used anymore, he found Votto's home address in a real-estate story, a puff piece about the young senator that was written before his daughter disappeared, before his wife died. He lived in the old Mansion District, where turn-of-the-century lumber barons had once resided. There was a picture of Votto standing by his pool, smiling, the sun in his eyes—*Life is beautiful.* Joe looked at the picture. Then he went out to a hardware store and picked up a new hammer.

Votto couldn't sleep. He lay in bed, twisting about. It was a little after three a.m.

He reached past his distended belly and touched his cock. Maybe if he came, he could sleep. But his cock was dead. Had been dead for months. He took hold of the pillow next to him, held it like it was a person. *I'm in hell,* he thought.

The people who owned him had put two men out back by the pool and two out front. Just a precaution, they said. It was more likely that McCleary's man, the ex-Marine, was halfway across the country, looking to hide. He wouldn't come to the bear. He'd run from it.

But still, just in case, they had sent the four men.

The two out front were sitting in their car, the engine running so they could stay warm, and Votto told the two out back they could use the fire pit. He felt like he was playing a role, pretending to be magnanimous and generous, worthy of guarding, but he could feel his veneer slipping. He could feel his face—his front to the world—melting, like someone burned alive in a horror movie.

Going from his side to his belly to his side, unable to tolerate his insomnia another second, he got out of bed. Wearing a T-shirt and boxer shorts, he went to the window and looked out at his pool. Its underwater lights were on, and it was luminous, a blue-liquid gem.

The guards had put the pool lights on to brighten the yard, to make it harder for an intruder, but Votto always found the lit-up pool to be beautiful and glamorous at night, even in this moment, and he felt pride at his ownership.

Then one of the men stepped into view, looking out at the lawn and the pool. Had he heard something? He cocked his head, listening. A cigarette dangled in his hand, the smoke pluming in the cold air. Then the man turned toward his unseen partner. He seemed to gesture, *It's nothing.* Then the man stepped out of sight, and Votto was back in hell.

But it wasn't just the specter of Joe that put him

there. It was all that he had done wrong, all that he had destroyed. He was not without conscience or what was left of one. He went to the master bathroom to look at the empty bottle of Xanax in the medicine cabinet. He had looked at it two hours before, but he unscrewed it again. Maybe somehow there was a pill he had missed. But of course there wasn't.

He put the bottle back on the shelf and stared at all the useless ointments and creams and odd medicine-cabinet detritus, almost all of it put there at one time by his wife. He imagined her standing there at the sink, opening the mirror, and for a moment it was as if she were right next to him. She had been his high school sweetheart, his best friend. *I killed her,* he thought.

He took out one of her moisturizers, unscrewed the cap, and held the tube to his nose. It had a vanilla scent. He used to love smelling that when he was at her nipple, along with the smell and taste of his own saliva. They both knew he liked the breast too much, but she forgave him for being a mama's boy. It made her feel loved.

Then he put the tube back and just stood there, trancelike, staring at all the useless crap he would never be able to throw away. Then something broke his trance—he saw a blue box that he hadn't noticed before; it had blended in with everything else. But now he remembered what it was. It was a box of codeine tablets his wife had bought in Paris on vacation. She liked codeine, said you couldn't get it in the States so easy. He tore open the box. There were four tablets left. He deciphered the French instructions—it said to take one. He figured three would put him to sleep but not kill him. He put them in his mouth, lowered his head to the sink, and gulped some water. He knew it couldn't work that quick, but he already felt tired.

He padded across the darkened room. He went to his wife's side and put on her old white-noise machine, which was still on her bedside table. The sound of ocean waves filled the room. He had never used the thing before—never liked it when she used it—but he was desperate.

Then he went and lay down on his side of the bed; he never roamed to her side. He curled into a fetal position, forced his eyes shut. But then the thinking started again.

How could he have done this to himself? He replayed it all for the millionth time. Each wrong move, each catastrophic choice.

His father's career had ended in scandal, but he'd been beloved for years—a thousand people had come to the funeral. So Votto felt that if he ran he could win, that there would be sympathy for the son. He was sure of it. The voters would want redemption for a man they had once admired. They'd want redemption for themselves. But Votto, an up-and-coming lawyer with his own small firm, couldn't finance a campaign. He needed money, backing, except nobody would touch him. Nobody would take the risk. They all thought it was too soon. But he couldn't wait. So he went to Long Island, to Bay Shore, to the men who had owned Votto Sr.

They listened to him, quiet and serious, and he felt respected. Then the boss, Novelli, a bald, squat man in his sixties with brutal hands, said he would do it. He'd put Votto in office, but Votto's daughter would have to pay for the campaign. Votto didn't understand. *What are you talking about?* So the boss explained it to him. They'd put the girl to work. This was the price. He could have her back after a year. *Maybe you'll be governor someday.*

What the boss didn't explain was that he had come to hate Votto's father in the years leading up to his death—his arrogance, his self-righteousness, his deluded belief that he actually served the people— and this was a way to spit on his grave by making his grandchild a whore. A whore he could have first. He had seen the child. She was beautiful, pristine. And after he had her, she'd pay for the campaign on her back. He liked the idea: its cruelty appealed to him. He was a sociopath—the source of his power—and a pedophile with grandchildren of his own. He didn't think Votto would say yes.

But he did say yes. Votto's father had always told him that you don't back down from a challenge, and this proposition had seemed like a challenge, a test of how much he wanted it, and he thought that once he said yes, the boss would take it back, reveal that he was only joking, just testing Votto's mettle.

Except Novelli wasn't joking. He was able to run New York for as long as he had because he was sick; the world and its laws didn't apply to him.

Votto tried to protest, but Novelli ended the meeting. He had other people to see.

Stunned, like he was sleepwalking, Votto left Bay Shore, leaving the deal in place. He didn't understand how he could be so weak. *I've lost everything*, he thought.

He spent the night in Manhattan, and the next day he went back, tried to undo it, this pact with the devil, but now the boss wanted the girl and wanted Votto in Albany. Votto begged him. *Please, I can't do this.* But the boss could taste it—the girl, the money, all of it—and there was no taking it back. He made it clear that if Votto resisted, he'd have him killed, make it look like an accident.

So Votto, a coward, gave them his daughter. He told himself that to be a great man in this world you had to be ruthless, even barbaric. You couldn't feel things the way normal people did; you had to be stronger. You had to be willing to sacrifice anything and anyone to get what you wanted, and what he wanted was power and to surpass his father. It's what he had always wanted.

But a month after Lisa's disappearance, his wife could tell that he was hiding something. She could see that he was acting, playing a role. Thinking that somehow she might understand and maybe share his burden, which he realized later was madness, he confessed to her.

He never saw anyone so transformed in an instant. He had a glimpse of her death mask.

Then she became hysterical and attacked him, raking her fingers across his neck. She said she was going to go to the Feds, the cops, somebody, but he stalled her long enough to make a call, and Novelli's people had her killed, made it look like a suicide. But he hadn't seen that coming. That wasn't why he called them, not consciously. He called because he was panicking. So they took care of it.

Somehow he kept going. *It was amazing*, he thought, *what you could live with, what you could hide.* Then that anonymous text had come, and suddenly he *couldn't* take it anymore. It was oddly more real than his wife's death, since there was a part of him that kept waiting for her to come home, as if none of this had hap-

pened. But the text was evidence of what he had done
to his daughter and to his wife, evidence of all that he
had destroyed.

Not knowing where else to go, he went to church
for the first time in years. He knelt on the cold floor and
prayed for help. It was an old Catholic church made of
flagstone with hundred-year-old wooden pews built
from the lumber that had once made Albany rich.

After a while, losing control, he crawled under the
pew in front of him—it was early in the morning,
and the church was empty. He began to weep, and he
spasmed on the stone floor, his body convulsing with
shame.

Then at the peak of this, Jesus said to him, *I forgive you, I can forgive anything*, and Votto felt a pro-
found relief. But then God spoke to him, commanded
him to make things right, and suddenly church made
sense to Votto. Jesus forgave you, but God was the law.
So, in a state of mania, he left the church and contacted McCleary. He'd get Lisa back and defy them,
defy Novelli. He put it all in motion. He hired that
ex-Marine. Sent him to get her.

But then he saw on the news that Wilson had
killed himself, and the frenzy that had come over him
in the church deserted him all at once.

He was sure in his gut that it had to be Wilson
who texted him. They were friends or pretended to
be friends, and Votto was one of the few people who

knew that Wilson had gone to rehab for drug addiction *and* sex addiction. But Votto never knew what *kind* of sex addiction.

He had hoped to punish whoever had texted him as a sacrificial lamb for all the other men who had raped his daughter, but now that person was dead and what had he been thinking, anyway? His ability to reason had returned and with it his inherent cowardice.

Defiance wasn't possible. Novelli would have him executed. And why get Lisa back? What was the point? There'd be nothing left of her. *Save yourself. What else can you do?*

So he let them ambush Joe and take Lisa back. They didn't like what he had done, but he was still of value to them, and they said they'd clean up his mess. Like with his wife.

That was last night. He hadn't slept for twenty-four hours. He waited for the codeine to take effect. He closed his eyes. *Please, God, let me sleep*, he prayed. *Please.* He was ready to believe again.

Then he heard the lamp next to his bed click on, and he opened his eyes and Joe was standing there. A gun, with a silencer, was in his hand.

Joe said, "I'd like to talk to you."

Hours earlier, Joe had gone to the hardware store, where he picked up a new hammer, latex gloves, duct tape, and a razor. From the hardware store, he went to a car-rental agency. He filled out the paperwork, and they gave him a drab green Ford that had all the style and shape of a cough drop.

He parked it at the hotel and went to rest. As he crossed the lobby, the girl at the desk smiled at him. Women responded to Joe. They could imagine how he would be in the dark.

In his room, he lay down and elevated his leg on a pillow. It seemed to help. He lay there for hours, inert, resting but not sleeping. Just once, he seemed to go under. It was like drowning, black and sudden. He felt fear and pulled himself out of it.

At 1:30 in the morning, wearing dark jeans and a black, hooded sweatshirt, Joe left the Hilton, using the emergency staircase, tilting his head away from a number of cameras. The hood helped to obscure his face, and the sweatshirt had two deep pockets, where he stashed McCleary's .45 and his purchases from the hardware store. In the waistband of his jeans, he tucked one of the silenced .22s.

By 1:45 he was at Votto's. The Mansion District was somber and dead, like a lot of old-money neighborhoods. There was the whiff of the mausoleum, of the well-tended graveyard. There were no streetlights, no sidewalks, and the houses were on a ridge, up a small incline from the road.

Votto's house was especially private, surrounded

by enormous box hedges twenty feet high and thick. The driveway sloped up the incline at a slight curve to the right for about thirty yards. Then it forked to the left to the garage but also kept going to the right where there was a circular turnaround in front of the house. Cars could park there or in the garage.

The house itself was morose and heavy, all red brick with several chimneys and four white columns framing the front door. There were neighbors to the right and left, but the hedges on all three sides made the house feel isolated, alone, and impenetrable.

Joe drove past the driveway at a normal speed and glanced up. At the top of the driveway in the turn-around was a car idling. Its headlights were on, and it faced the street, lighting up the driveway and the approach to the house. He could see the exhaust swirling, white smoke in the late October air.

So they *had* anticipated that he might come. There must be guards of some type sitting in that car, and they were using the car's lights to illuminate the front yard and the driveway like floodlights in a prison yard.

Joe drove around the area to see if there might be a way in through the back. But the roads were winding and serpentine, the properties for each house fairly large, and it was impossible to know exactly which house was behind Votto's and what barriers he might encounter. Also, the houses around here would have half-decent security systems, maybe even motion detectors. He didn't have time to case things; the best way, the simplest way, would be through the front.

He left the Ford two streets over from Votto's where there were some other cars parked on the road. Most of the houses were dark, with scattered lights on here and there. It was a cloudy, overcast night, and without streetlights, it was nearly pitch black.

Joe, despite his wounded leg, walked rapidly to the edge of Votto's property, stopping about one hundred feet to the right of the driveway. The hedges acted like a wall around a castle, but they also kept Joe from being seen by whoever was guarding the front of the house.

There were no cars parked on Votto's street, which meant they hadn't placed anyone on the far perimeter, only the near perimeter. Either they had underestimated the risk or they were stupid. Joe didn't care. Both were good for him. He was fairly certain there would be two in the car. He wondered if there might be more inside or in the back. But he knew to keep things simple, to follow the straight line. Take out whoever was in the car and go from there.

There was no way through the hedge except to drop to the ground and go along at the roots like a small animal. He transferred the .22, the .45, and the hammer to the back of his pants, tucking everything in by his tailbone. The duct tape, razor, and gloves stayed in his pockets.

The first bit was the most worrisome, should a car drive by. But the darkness gave him good cover, and he moved quickly, ripping at the hedges with his hands.

The main, thick roots, which he couldn't tear out, were about a foot apart. But that was just enough room for him to make his way through, narrowing his body and edging along on his side, while breaking the thinner branches off and clearing the way. The branches scratched his face and his hands, but he didn't care. And no cars passed. The rich were sleeping.

After less than a minute, he got far enough so that he was able to pull his legs through. Now he was completely hidden from the road or the house. He stopped for a moment, rested, and then continued. The hedges were about seven feet thick.

He wasn't worried that the sound of his movements would reach the car. He was about forty yards away, across the lawn, and the idling engine would block out any noise. As he neared the end, where the hedge met the lawn, he could see the car illuminated by a light over the front door. It was a four-door black Cadillac with elaborate rims.

Goons, Joe thought, and he rested again, putting the side of his face in the dirt. It was cool and felt good, but his bad leg was pounding. Then he looked back up. The driver's side of the Caddy was facing Joe, but he could make out that two were in the car, and the driver's window was cracked ever so slightly so that the windows wouldn't fog up.

The headlights of the car were pointing down the curved driveway to the left, so Joe figured he could crawl up the right-hand side of the lawn, which was completely dark, without being seen.

Then he'd come at the car from behind, but he didn't think he could take them silently. If he crawled up to the driver's-side door, opened it, and went at them with the .22, it could work. But if the door was locked, it would get loud very quickly, and shooting them through the window with the .45 would be useless. He'd never get to Votto.

He was going to have to wait for one or both of them to get out of the car to either stretch their legs or take a piss. That would make things easier. He looked at his watch. It was 2:10. He had at least three hours of darkness. He could wait. But he wanted to be in position. He emerged from the hedge and, staying on his belly, crawled up the slope of the lawn to the shrubs along the front of the house.

He was now behind the car about thirty feet away. The car was parked parallel to the front door and faced the street. Joe stayed flat to the ground, put on a pair of the latex gloves, and got the .22 in his hand. They wouldn't be able to see him in the rearview mirror. The light over the front door didn't have a wide arc, and there was no light spill coming from inside the house. The windows were black.

He looked at his gloved hands. Did it matter any-more if he left prints? Everything had changed. He no longer had a home. What was he protecting? But then Joe thought it best to stick to his pattern, to what had always worked, like wearing gloves, and he dismissed these thoughts from his mind.

And as he staked them out, Joe experienced, as he often did in such situations, a feeling of peace, an exquisite state of focus and concentration. He was unaware of the cold or the throbbing in his leg. He was poised, weightless, not quite in his body yet wholly present. When they made a move, he would know what to do. The world felt simple. Minutes passed eas-ily without struggle.

But then, without warning, his mind betrayed him. He saw the burnt hole the bullet had made in his mother's head, and he was back in the room with her, lifting the pillow off her face. Then that moment kept repeating itself on a loop, and he was blind in the real world. He couldn't see the car. He wasn't on the lawn. He was in her room. Lifting the pillow. The scorched hole. Her corpse.

The opening of the passenger's-side door snapped him out of it. A large man with a shaved head got out, slammed the door, and went directly into the house. Joe, staying low and in the shadows, ran to the car, opened the passenger door, and was going to shoot the man inside, but he hesitated.

The man stared at Joe and muttered, "What the fuck?" Then he got over his shock and started to reach for one of the guns—there were two—on the dashboard. But Joe moved fast, slid into the passenger seat, and with the butt of the .22 chopped the man in the throat.

The man, bearded and built wide like a refrigerator, began to choke violently. Joe put the .22 on the dash and pulled the man toward him. He crossed his forearms against the man's neck while grabbing the underside of his collar with both hands. He then brought the man close to his chest and squeezed, making a vise with his forearms and the collar of the jacket.

This cross choke put Joe's bony wrists, which were like the knobs of baseball bats, against the man's carotid arteries. The man thrashed, but Joe put him to sleep like a child in ten seconds. Then he released him, propping him against the driver's-side window. Joe glanced at the clock on the dashboard. It was 3:03. It hadn't felt like it, but he had staked them out for nearly an hour, and the bald one had gone inside about thirty seconds ago.

Using the duct tape, he quickly lashed the man's neck to the headrest, gagged his mouth, and bound his hands and feet. He wouldn't be going anywhere. The other one had been inside for at least ninety seconds. Joe decided to take him in the house. Didn't want to risk it in front of the door should a car drive by.

Joe then grabbed the two guns on the dash and his .22. He got out of the car, threw their guns in the bushes, and opened the front door. The .22 in his hand, he went in low, crouching, since they'd expect him to come in standing and aim for the head, but no one was there and he stepped into a darkened foyer. There was some light coming from an upstairs hall-way and down a carpeted staircase, which was about ten feet from the door and to the left.

At the end of the foyer was a door, and some light was coming out from beneath it. Joe heard water run-ning. He moved quickly to the door, opened it, and the bald goon turned from the sink. Joe shot him in the knee, and the man crumpled. The .22 was good for close-range work.

Before the bald man could make a noise, Joe was on him, this time doing a rear choke, since there was more room in the bathroom than in the car. After he put the man to sleep, he gagged and trussed him with the duct tape and made a tourniquet for his leg.

But he didn't understand what he was doing. Why didn't he kill the one in the car and this one? It was more efficient to kill them. He was putting himself at risk taking so much time. He had brought the tape with him only because it was part of the pattern, the routine. He didn't think he'd use it. Then he was back in his mother's room, lifting the pillow.

I'm not functioning right, he thought, and he looked in the mirror, which was a good thing to do. He hated his face, and it brought him back to reality.

He stepped quietly out of the bathroom. Gun in front, leading the way, he crossed the foyer and went into the darkened living room. It was long and narrow with show furniture that still looked new, and it led to a dining room. Off the dining room, there were French doors. Outside the doors, Joe could make out two men sitting by a fire pit. Their backs were to him. Beyond them was a glowing pool.

He moved soundlessly to the French doors and opened them. He said, "Stand up. Slow."

The two men turned in their chairs and saw his gun. They looked like brothers. Dark and loose-limbed. Probably good fighters. The one on the right looked meaner and older. Their jackets bulged with guns.

"You motherfucker," said the one on the right.

Joe leveled the gun at his head. "Stand up," Joe said.

They both stood, eyeing him. "I'm going to kill you," said the one on the right. He was the spokesman.

"Where's Votto?" Joe said, keeping the gun on both of them now.

"Fuck you," said the talker, but the one on the left glanced up at the second story of the house. Joe stepped around them and glanced up at the house, then stepped back out of the windows' sight line. He didn't see anybody in the windows up there, and the fire pit, tucked to the right, wasn't visible from above. Votto must be up there, probably asleep. Joe waved the gun.

"Facedown on the ground and spread your legs."

The one on the left dropped to the ground, but the one on the right made a pathetic reach for his gun like a cowboy, and Joe shot him in the thigh. "Fuck," he said, almost quietly, in shock, never having been shot before. He fell to his knees, and Joe moved in and clipped him on the back of the head with the .22. Now he was facedown on the ground.

The other one didn't move. He did as he was told. He'd been arrested more than once; he knew the drill.

"You're smart," Joe said to him.

"I try to be." His voice was muffled.

"That's right. No reason to die tonight. Your two friends out front are still alive."

The man grunted.

"Any more of you in the house?" Joe was angled so he could see in through the French doors.

The man didn't answer. Joe put the barrel of the .22 in the man's ear.

"Any more of you in the house?"

"Just the four of us."

"And where's Votto?"

"Upstairs."

"Sleeping?"

The man shrugged. Joe then got out the tape and the razor, gagged him, secured him and his partner, and made a tourniquet for the wounded man. He took their guns.

He went back inside and checked the other downstairs rooms. He didn't think the compliant one had been lying but better to be sure. The rooms were empty. He hid their guns under the sink in the kitchen.

He then went to the foyer and up the staircase. He figured Votto was asleep, but he could be waiting for Joe. He could have a gun.

The upstairs hallway was dimly lit, just one fake sconce in the middle of the wall. He passed a girl's bedroom—Lisa's, still intact—a bathroom, a study, and then at the end of the hall was a partially open door. There was no light coming from that room, but he could hear the sounds of the ocean, which made no sense to Joe.

He peered inside the room—the ocean sounds were loud, and he realized it was some kind of sleeping-aid machine. He could make out the form of a body on the far left side of the bed; its back was to him. Joe walked in quietly, turned on the lamp next to the body, and Votto's eyes opened. Joe pointed the .22 at him and said, "I'd like to talk to you."

"Don't kill me," Votto said. It came out of his mouth before he even thought it.

Joe sat on the edge of the bed, like a doctor making a house call. He kept the gun on Votto, studied him.

Votto scooted back into a half-sitting position against the bedstead, scared. Joe's hands in the rubber gloves terrified him.

Then Joe spoke. "Where's Lisa?"

Votto didn't say anything. He couldn't think straight. *How do I get out of this?*

Joe repeated the question. "Where's Lisa?"

"Are you . . . are you going to kill me?"

"Not if you answer my questions."

Votto stared at him. Maybe he was telling the truth.

"Where's Lisa?"

"She . . . they took her to Philadelphia."

"Where in Philadelphia?"

"They said it was a place called the farm. They said she'd be okay there."

Votto's face was flushed and corpulent. *He looks like a human pig*, Joe thought.

"Where's the farm?"

"They didn't tell me. I swear."

Joe was silent. *Philadelphia.* He'd go there first. That's where the new line would begin.

"Are you going to kill me?"

Joe ignored that. "When they kidnapped Lisa, why didn't you go to the cops?"

Votto looked away.

"Why didn't you?"

Votto was silent.

"Look at me."

With his left hand, Joe grabbed Votto's face, digging his fingers into the skin of his cheeks, and turned his head forward. Votto's eyes met Joe's. Joe kept the gun on Votto's gut. "Why didn't you go to the cops?"

Votto blinked. But wouldn't talk. Joe wouldn't let him turn his head; his hand was like an iron clamp.

Joe said, "Tell me."

Votto shook his head. Joe took the .22 and worked it into Votto's mouth.

Votto choked, and Joe shoved it further down his throat. Then he drew the gun out slow and pressed it hard against Votto's forehead. The barrel was wet with saliva.

"Tell me."

Votto broke. "I didn't go to the cops because I made a deal. You understand? A fucking deal."

Joe didn't get it at first and then he did, and he let go of Votto's face, pushing him away in disgust. Joe, in his figuring on the train, had gotten just about everything right, except this—the mob hadn't gone to Votto; he'd gone to them.

Joe stood, keeping the gun on Votto.

"Who did you make the deal with?"

Votto turned away again, like a petulant child.

"I told you I won't kill you if you talk to me. You want to live, right? Who'd you make the deal with?"

"Novelli." He said it in a whisper.

"Where do I find Novelli?"

"Bay Shore." Another whisper.

Philadelphia, Bay Shore. That was the line. He just had to follow the line.

Joe put the .22 in his pocket. Votto couldn't believe it. Maybe he *was* going to live. Maybe he could find a new wife, have another child, start over, make everything right. He saw it in a flash.

Joe took out his new hammer. Votto thought, *Why does he have a hammer?*

Then Joe lifted it into the air, and Votto had his answer.

Joe sunk the hammer deep into Votto's forehead and left it there. He wanted them to know he was coming.

SEXUAL METAMORPHOSIS
An Anthology of Transsexual Memoirs

In *Sexual Metamorphosis*, Jonathan Ames presents the personal narratives of fifteen gender pioneers. Here is Christine Jorgensen, the first celebrity transsexual, greeting thousands of well-wishers from the stage of Madison Square Garden. Here is Caroline Cossey, former model and Bond (as in James) girl, being outed in the tabloid press. Here is novelist and English professor Jennifer Finney Boylan discussing her impending transformation with her heartbroken spouse and supportive yet confused colleagues. The result is a fascinating and compulsively readable book, filled with anguish, introspection, and courage.

Gender Studies

WHAT'S NOT TO LOVE?
The Adventures of a Mildly Perverted Young Writer

This wonderfully entertaining memoir is a touching and humorous look at life in New York City. But this is life for an author who can proclaim "my first sexual experience was rather old-fashioned: it was with a prostitute"—an author who can talk about his desire to be a model for the Hair Club for Men and about meeting his son for the first time. Often insightful, sometimes tender, always witty and self-deprecating, *What's Not to Love?* is an engaging memoir from one of our most funny, most daring writers.

Memoir

VINTAGE BOOKS
Available wherever books are sold.
www.vintagebooks.com